To our "mob"
Lyndal & Paul, Leanne & Mat

Space story idea from Class 1/2 HW (2006)
Lavington East Public School

Published in 2010 by Windmill Books, LLC
303 Park Avenue South, Suite # 1280, New York, NY 10010-3657

Originally published by JoJo Publishing
"Yarra's Edge"
2203/80 Lorimer Street
Docklands VIC 3008
Australia

In conjunction with Purple Pig Productions

CREDITS:
Text by Alan Bowater
Illustrated by Pete Pascoe
Designed by Pete Pascoe, Alan Bowater, and Rob Ryan

Publisher Cataloging Data

Bowater, Alan
A sheep called Sean. – North American ed. / written by Alan Bowater ; illustrated by Pete Pascoe.
p. cm. – (A pig called Pete)
Summary: When Pete the flying pig meets Sean the sheep, they learn that sometimes friends say hurtful things they don't really mean.
ISBN 978-1-60754-570-5 (lib.) – ISBN 978-1-60754-571-2 (pbk.)
ISBN 978-1-60754-572-9 (6-pack)
1. Friendship—Juvenile fiction 2. Swine—Juvenile fiction 3. Sheep—Juvenile fiction [1. Friendship—Fiction 2. Pigs—Fiction 3. Sheep—Fiction 4. Planets—Fiction] I. Pascoe, Pete II. Title: Pig called Pete meets-- a sheep called Sean III. Title IV. Series
[E]—dc22

Printed in the United States of America

For more great fiction and nonfiction, visit windmillbooks.com.

A Sheep Called Sean

Written by Alan Bowater Illustrated by Pete Pascoe

an imprint of
WINDMILL BOOKS™
New York

One day my pig called Pete met Sean.
A sheep called Sean.

He was hiding in a box!

Sean’s a smart sheep who sings.

He’s a “baaritone”!

Sean sings in the shower. No? Yes.

Sean sings in the bathtub. No? Yes.

Sean sings all the time! No? Yes.

Sean and Pete built a spaceship from boxes.

They tied it up with string.

It's got a computer and two booster rockets!

Sean and Pete shut their eyes!

The earth gets smaller and smaller.

They wave to the man in the moon.

They pass Mercury, the hot planet

and Venus, the evening star.

They pass Mars, the red planet

and Jupiter, the giant planet.

Then, they pass Saturn, the planet with rings

and Uranus, the mysterious planet!

They pass Neptune, the aqua planet.

Soon, they reach Pluto, a dwarf planet.

Pete lands on Pluto!

Sean follows.

It’s freezing!

Pete’s teeth chatter. Sean’s knees knock.

Sean and Pete
play polo

and putt-putt golf

and Ping-Pong

and pole vaulting.
Pete wins!

But Sean says, "Pete's a cheat!"

Pete feels hurt and heads home to me.

I'm dreaming about Pete and me being pirates.
We're sailing the seas searching for a ship to scuttle.

Pete crawls under my bed.

In the morning Pete tells me he's not a cheat.

I tell Pete that sometimes friends say hurtful things they don't really mean.

On Pluto, Sean's sorry for what he said.

He hopes the spaceship will come back soon.

While Sean waits he sees Halley's comet
and a shooting star.

Sean makes a wish!

Then, from the darkness of space a ship appears.

It's Pete!

He lands beside Sean with a great big grin!

They zoom toward Earth, the water planet –

home sweet home!